CURRENT
SCIENCE®

SUPERHERO SCIENCE

Kapow! Comic Book Crime Fighters Put Physics to the Test

By Lynnette Brent Sandvold and Barbara Bakowski

Reading Adviser: Cecilia Minden-Cupp, Ph.D., Literacy Consultant
Science Curriculum Content Consultant: Debra Voege, M.A.

Gareth Stevens
Publishing

Please visit our web site at **www.garethstevens.com**.
For a free color catalog describing Gareth Stevens Publishing's list of
high-quality books, call 1-800-542-2595 (USA) or 1-800-387-3178 (Canada).
Gareth Stevens Publishing's fax: 1-877-542-2596

Library of Congress Cataloging-in-Publication Data
Sandvold, Lynnette Brent.
    Superhero science : kapow! comic book crime fighters put physics to the test /
    by Lynnette Brent Sandvold and Barbara Bakowski ; reading consultant,
    Cecilia Minden-Cupp ; science curriculum content consultant, Debra Voege.
        p. cm. — (Current science)
    Includes bibliographical references and index.
    ISBN-10: 1-4339-2243-6   ISBN-13: 978-1-4339-2243-5 (lib. bdg.)
    1. Science—Juvenile literature. 2. Science fiction in science education—
Juvenile literature. I. Bakowski, Barbara. II. Title.
Q163.S19   2010
500—dc22   2009011403

This edition first published in 2010 by
Gareth Stevens Publishing
A Weekly Reader® Company
1 Reader's Digest Road
Pleasantville, NY 10570-7000 USA

Copyright © 2010 by Gareth Stevens, Inc.

Current Science™ is a trademark of Weekly Reader Corporation. Used under license.

Gareth Stevens Executive Managing Editor: Lisa M. Herrington
Gareth Stevens Senior Editor: Barbara Bakowski
Gareth Stevens Cover Designer: Keith Plechaty

Created by **Q2AMedia**
Editor: Jessica Cohn
Art Director: Rahul Dhiman
Designer: Harleen Mehta
Photo Researcher: Kamal Kumar
Illustrator: Ashish Tanwar

Photo credits (t = top; b = bottom; c = center; l = left; r = right):
Warner Bros./Courtesy Everett Collection (Batman and Superman), 20th Century Fox Film Corp./Courtesy
Everett Collection (Invisible Woman): cover, Marvel/Sony Pictures/The Kobal Collection: title page,
Columbia/Marvel/The Kobal Collection: 4, Inc Superstock/Photolibrary: 5, Warner Bros./DC Comics/
The Kobal Collection: 6, Istockphoto: 7t, 20th Century Fox/The Kobal Collection: 8, Joe McDonald/Corbis:
9t, Daniel Heuclin/NHPA: 9b, Columbia/Marvel/The Kobal Collection: 10, Simon Holdcroft/Alamy: 11,
20th Century Fox/Marvel Entertainment/The Kobal Collection/Israelson, Nels: 12, FogScreen: 13,
Ronald Grant Archive: 14, Lee Prince/Shutterstock: 15, Warner Bros./DC Comics/The Kobal Collection:
16t, Q2AMedia Image Bank: 16bl, Argonaut/Shutterstock: 16br, 20th Century Fox/The Kobal Collection:
17t, NASA/JPL-Caltech: 17bl, Rex Features: 17br, Capital Pictures: 18, Win McNamee/Staff/Getty Images:
19, Rex Features: 20, RIA Novosti/Alamy: 21t, Brandi Simons/Stringer/Getty Images: 21b, Barcroft
Media: 22, Shawn Rocco/Associated Press: 23t, Adrees Latif/Reuters: 23b, Marvel Enterprises/The Kobal
Collection: 24, Istockphoto: 25t, Photobucket.com, Inc.: 25b, Capital Pictures: 26, Dreamstime: 27, Marvel
Enterprises/The Kobal Collection: 28-29, www.army.mil: 28r, Marvel/Sony Pictures/The Kobal Collection:
30, Craigdingle/Dreamstime: 31, Julián Rovagnati/Shutterstock: 32t, Dario Sabljak/Shutterstock: 32c,
U.S. Department of Energy Artificial Retina Project: 33, 20th Century Fox/Marvel Ent. Group/The Kobal
Collection/Dory, Attila: 34, Jim Zuckerman/Corbis: 36, Asther Lau Choon Siew/Dreamstime: 37t, Shizuo
Kambayashi/Associated Press: 37b, Iudex/Istockphoto: 38, David B. Fleetham/Photolibrary: 38-39, Warner
Bros./DC Comics/The Kobal Collection: 40, 20th Century Fox/Courtesy Everett Collection: 41, Capital
Pictures: 42, Kevin Fisher: 44, Q2AMedia Image Bank: 47
Q2AMedia Art Bank: 7, 15, 27, 31, 32, 33, 35, 43, 45

Printed in the United States of America
1 2 3 4 5 6 7 8 9 12 11 10 09

CONTENTS

Words in **boldface** type are defined in the glossary.

Chapter 1

SUPER IN EVERY WAY

We love our comic book, TV, and movie superheroes. These characters have amazing abilities. Some of their superpowers are out of this world. Many, however, are based in real-life science.

Real-life heroes use brains, courage, and the tools of their trade to help others.

DIAL 9

WHAT IS A SUPERHERO?

Some real-life people are superheroes. Firefighters and police officers, for instance, risk their lives to keep people safe. Doctors work to prevent and cure diseases. Teachers encourage and inspire students.

Fictional superheroes are bigger than life, though. Their powers may include superhuman strength, supersharp senses, or the ability to fly. Some superheroes can become invisible. Others use technology to travel through time or move with superspeed.

Some superheroes are born with their amazing powers. Others have accidents that cause them to change.

The Hulk, for example, was changed by harmful **radiation**. Spider-Man's powers came from a **radioactive** spider bite.

SCIENCE—OR SCIENCE FICTION?

Although superheroes gain their powers in different ways, most of their stories are rooted in science. In fact, many superheroes and the villains they fight are scientists. The Hulk is **nuclear physicist** Bruce Banner. Mr. Fantastic, of the Fantastic Four, is a scientist and an engineer.

Find out how superheroes use real-life science and modern technology to save the world!

Chapter 2

Up, Up, AND AWAY!

Superman came to Earth from a planet called Krypton. This high-flying hero is "faster than a speeding bullet." But you don't have to hail from Krypton to have the power of flight. People and animals here on Earth can fly by using the forces of nature.

FLYING HIGH

With airplane power, humans can overcome **gravity**. Gravity is the pull of Earth on objects near its surface. A strong engine also helps a plane overcome **drag**. That is a force that slows an object as it moves through air. Air pushes back against the moving object.

The speed of a plane's engine works with the wind moving across its wings. The engine creates a force called **thrust**. Thrust helps the airplane push through drag. As the plane speeds up, the air over the top of its wings moves faster than the air below the wings. This difference creates a force called **lift**. Lift helps the plane pull away from Earth's gravity. All these forces combine to make airplane flight possible.

World's Fastest Bird

The peregrine falcon has been called nature's finest flying machine. This bird can fly as fast as 200 miles (322 kilometers) per hour. A peregrine falcon flies fastest when it is hunting a mouse or another meal. The falcon dives toward the ground, grabs its dinner, flaps its wings, and returns to normal flight.

FAST FACT

The first powered airplane flight lasted only 12 seconds. In 1903, Orville Wright flew 120 feet (37 meters) in a craft he built with his brother Wilbur.

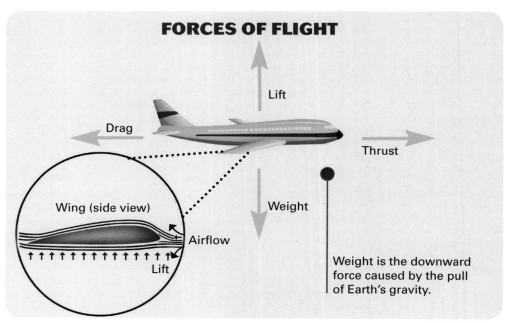

FORCES OF FLIGHT

Lift

Drag

Thrust

Weight

Wing (side view)

Airflow

Lift

Weight is the downward force caused by the pull of Earth's gravity.

A MIGHTY WIND

Storm is a member of the X-Men team. Her superpowers enable her to change the weather. She can make rain, create fog, or cause lightning strikes. Storm also has the ability to raise and lower the temperature. She can make powerful winds blow.

Storm is able to fly by creating winds strong enough to support her. She can even carry other people along. She can travel as fast and as far as any wind can travel.

Andrea Thomas was a 1970s TV superhero who could also fly. With a cry of "Oh, mighty Isis!" she became the ancient Egyptian goddess Isis. Winds lifted her into the air. Isis then flew off to stop criminals and save lives.

Storm uses the power of wind for flight.

When at rest, the flying squirrel's skin flaps fold against its body.

FURRY FLYERS

Like Storm and Isis, some animals are carried by the wind. Have you ever heard of a flying squirrel? What about a sugar glider? Those animals appear to fly through the air. They do not fly as birds do, however.

As their name suggests, sugar gliders glide through the air. Flying squirrels do the same thing. Both animals have a thin piece of skin stretched between their arms and legs. When the animals leap from high places, the skin flaps work like sails. They catch the wind to hold the animals up.

Strange but True

The flying tree snake cannot fly or glide, but it still can travel through the air. Its body forms a sort of parachute. The shape traps air and slows the snake's fall. The snake wiggles its body to steer while in the air!

On his bat-shaped glider, the evil Green Goblin sets out to destroy Spider-Man.

PERSONAL FLYING DEVICES

Some superheroes count on devices that help them get around. The Silver Surfer, for example, has a super surfboard. A regular surfboard works on water. The Silver Surfer's board flies through the air. He can travel at top speeds, even into space! The Silver Surfer races to help people in need.

Bad guys have cool aircraft, too. The Green Goblin has a "goblin glider" powered by a superstrong fan. The villain's glider can reach a speed of 300 miles (483 km) per hour. Now, that's fast! Watch out, Spider-Man!

CROSSING A CANYON

Today, inventors and engineers are turning comic book technology into reality. In 2008, stuntman Eric Scott used a jet pack to fly across a canyon. The canyon was 1,500 feet (457 m) wide. The pack could carry only a certain amount of fuel. When Scott landed, he had only nine seconds' worth of fuel to spare. The fuel was hydrogen peroxide. You might know that substance as hair bleach!

REACHING NEW HEIGHTS

A New Zealand company makes a flying device that carries one rider. This machine has two gasoline-powered fans to create lift. The pack can lift a person 8,000 feet (2,438 m) above the ground for as long as 30 minutes.

FAST FACT
Powered hang gliders are launched by foot and then run on engines. These devices give hang gliders more "air time."

Stuntman Eric Scott uses a jet pack to fly at 75 miles (121 km) per hour.

WHAT DO YOU THINK?
What future inventions might improve personal flying devices?

Chapter 3

Beyond
FLIGHT

Have you ever wished you could just think about a place and instantly be there? Nightcrawler can. Superheroes who lack the power of flight have other, amazing ways to

Light bounces off a fog screen to create an image in thin air.

WALKING THROUGH WALLS

Like Nightcrawler, Kitty Pryde of the X-Men can **teleport**. She shifts her **atoms** through the spaces between the atoms of a solid object. In that way, she can pass through something solid, such as a wall.

These shifts and movements are similar to a process called tunneling. Tunneling allows tiny particles to pass through barriers. Your computer, your cell phone, some microscopes, and other gadgets work because of tunneling. As fantastic as it sounds, it's real-world physics!

Floating in Air

Inspired by science fiction, inventors have found a way to make people and objects appear out of thin air! Tap water, fans, and superfast **sound waves** create a thin curtain of tiny water droplets in the air. Images are then projected, or shone, onto the screen of fog. The droplets are so tiny, you can walk through the "wall" of pictures without feeling wet. The inventors of the technology say they wanted to re-create sci-fi movie effects in real life.

13

FROM FICTION TO FACT

"Beam me up, Scotty!" That famous line is from the sci-fi TV series *Star Trek*. Scotty is the chief engineer in the stories. He teleports Captain Kirk and the rest of the *Enterprise* crew from place to place.

Star Trek used film tricks to show teleportation. In real life, people "teleport" things every day. When someone sends a fax or an e-mail, a copy of an object is made. Then it is sent to a new location and re-created there.

E-mails and faxes do not happen in an instant, so they are not true examples of teleportation. A team of scientists did carry out real teleportation recently, however. They sent information between two atoms about 3.3 feet (1 m) apart.

Are you hoping for a teleporter that can beam you from math class to recess? The experts say you will have a long wait!

TRULY MAGNETIC

Magneto, an enemy of the X-Men, has the power to control **magnetism**. In real life, the same force keeps a refrigerator door closed and helps a TV or computer monitor work properly. Magnets power **MRI** machines, used by doctors to see inside the body. MRI machines provide detailed images of body structures and functions.

A maglev train uses magnetism, too. *Mag* is short for "magnets." *Lev* is short for "levitation." Levitation is the act of rising, as if not affected by gravity. A maglev train levitates with magnetism.

The opposite ends of magnets attract each other. Ends that are the same repel, or push away, each other. A maglev train works because a magnetized track repels large magnets on the underside of the train. The train actually floats over special rails. Powerful magnets attract and repel parts of the train, moving the vehicle forward. Because maglev trains float on air, they are not slowed by **friction** between metal wheels and rails.

Maglev trains travel twice as fast as regular trains that run on steel tracks.

YOU DO IT!
Master Magnetism

What You Need
- 3 donut magnets
- dowel rod

What You Do
Step 1
Place the magnets on the dowel rod, held vertically. Which sides of the magnets are attracted to each other?

Step 2
Try to have the magnets repel each other. Flip the magnets as needed.

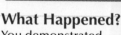

Step 3
Try to keep one magnet suspended above the other. Move the magnets up and down on the dowel rod to make this happen.

What Happened?
You demonstrated magnetic levitation, the force used in maglev trains.

SUPERPOWERS ON EARTH

Superman is one of the most powerful superheroes. The Man of Steel can even fly faster than the speed of light!

How Fast Does It Travel?

Light	983,571,056 feet (299,792,458 m) per second
Space rocket	36,959 feet (11,265 m) per second
Bullet	About 2,953 feet (900 m) per second
Concorde jet	1,125 feet (343 m) per second
Sound	1,116 feet (340 m) per second
Running cheetah	98 feet (30 m) per second

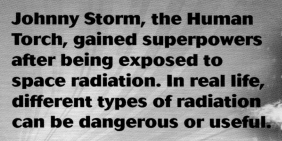

Johnny Storm, the Human Torch, gained superpowers after being exposed to space radiation. In real life, different types of radiation can be dangerous or useful.

Radiation: A Bad Rap?

Not all kinds of radiation are bad. Radiation can be used to:

- diagnose and treat illnesses
- kill germs and preserve food
- make smoke detectors, nonstick frying pans, and even ice cream!
- power **satellites**
- measure air pollution
- find the age of ancient objects

Storm can control the weather. In real life, the weather is something scientists try to predict.

Tools for Weather Prediction

- Barometers measure air pressure.
- Anemometers measure the speed of wind.
- Wind vanes show the wind's direction.
- Psychrometers show the amount of humidity in air.
- Thermometers measure temperature.
- Weather satellites monitor Earth's weather and climate from space.

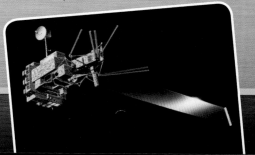

Chapter 4

A Few Extra PARTS

Dr. Octopus is one of Spider-Man's most sinister enemies. Thanks to an experiment gone wrong, Doc Ock has four extra limbs. He controls the mechanical arms with his brain. In real life, a person who is missing a hand, an arm, or a leg can be fitted with a high-tech replacement.

SUPER LIMBS

Scientists, doctors, and engineers work together to make artificial limbs called **prostheses**. These manufactured parts replace injured or missing legs, hands, or arms. The medical devices let people lead active lives.

High-tech legs have computers to help the wearer stay balanced. A computer can adjust an artificial leg 50 times a second! A computer helps move the ankle, too. One type of manufactured leg has a wireless remote control. It lets users switch settings for different activities, such as biking and skating.

Doctors can even take nerves from a lost limb to help move a prosthetic

Extreme Makeover

Jaime Sommers, TV's **Bionic** Woman, got high-tech body parts after a car accident. Bionic legs, an arm, an ear, and an eye gave her superstrength, superspeed, and other abilities. That is some serious girl power!

limb. The doctors attach the nerves to another body muscle. The nerves send electrical signals to operate the mechanical limb. When the brain thinks about making a movement, the nerves and the machinery work together to carry it out.

The user's mind controls the action of the prosthetic arm and hand.

19

MATERIAL MAN

Another character with extra parts is Wolverine, one of the X-Men. He has a special skeleton. A superstrong metal is bonded to his bones. He has six sharp metal claws that shoot out of his knuckles. The claws easily cut through most materials. Believe it or not, Wolverine's super-skeleton is more science than fiction.

Wolverine's razor-sharp metal claws come in handy when he faces off against enemies.

SKIN AND BONE

In real-world medicine, doctors use special metals to fix broken bones. They use rods, screws, and pins to hold the bone in place. Some artificial body parts, such as hip joints, are made of strong metal.

With lifelike materials, replacement hands can be matched to a person's skin coloring. An artificial hand can have fingernails, hairs, and pores (tiny holes in skin).

Researchers in California have created an artificial muscle that heals itself and makes electricity, too! Those super muscles change **chemical energy** into **mechanical energy**—just as natural muscles do.

Strange but True

Robert Heinlein was one of the greatest sci-fi authors of all time. More than 50 years ago, he wrote about things that have since been invented.

In "Waldo," Heinlein wrote about robotic devices controlled by humans. People now use similar devices to handle dangerous materials and to perform surgery. The devices are known as "waldoes," after the character in Heinlein's story. Reading science fiction may help us better understand the science of the future!

Wolverine's claws are cool, but this bionic hand is amazing! Each finger is powered by its own motor.

A prosthetic tail helps Winter, a dolphin, steer in water.

WINTER'S TAIL

Prosthetic limbs are not just for people. Animals have been fitted with fake limbs, too. Winter is a bottlenose dolphin at a Florida aquarium. She is one of the world's most famous dolphins. Why? She has a prosthetic tail! Winter lost her tail in a fish trap. Yet caretakers did not lose hope. They took Winter to the aquarium. There, experts on prostheses fitted her with a new tail. Winter can swim with the other dolphins again. She makes a big splash with visitors, too.

EXCEPTIONAL ELEPHANT

Motala is an Asian elephant. Asian elephants are special because few of them are left in the wild. Yet Motala is more special than most. She has a prosthetic limb.

Motala's home country is Thailand. She was hurt when a land mine exploded there. With her injured foot, Motala would have died in the wild. Animal doctors and other experts created a leg for her, however. Today, Motala walks much as a normal elephant does. She has made it possible for other injured elephants to receive such limbs.

A New Leash on Life

Cassidy, a three-legged dog, is famous. Animal doctors placed a metal fitting into his right back leg bone. Over the next few months, the metal part fused, or connected, with Cassidy's bone. Then an artificial leg was screwed onto the metal part. Cassidy now enjoys walks on four legs. This dog may truly be "man's best friend." He helped doctors learn things that might aid humans who lose or injure limbs.

Motala, an Asian elephant, can walk normally with an artificial leg.

Chapter 5

MUTATIONS and Adaptations

Superheroes are different from "regular" folks. In superhero stories, some characters gain their powers when their bodies are changed by radiation. Would you want to have mutant powers of your own? In some ways, you already do!

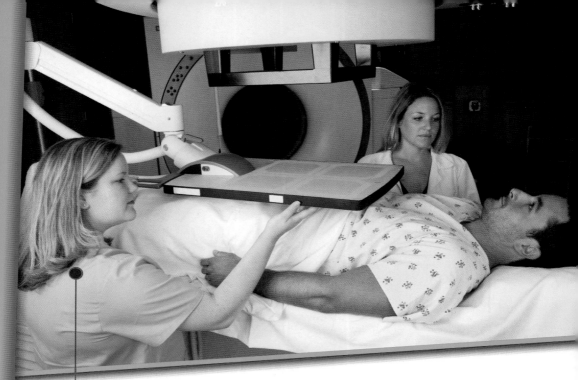

Doctors can use radiation to treat cancer.

ME, A MUTANT?

Mutations are changes in a living thing's **genes**. Genes in the body's **cells** decide the characteristics of a living thing. Mutations happen naturally in every cell of the body. So, in a way, every person is a mutant!

GOOD RAYS, BAD RAYS

Mutations can be caused by something in the environment, such as radiation. The Hulk became a mutant when he was hit with **gamma rays** from a nuclear reaction. When particles in the **nucleus** of an atom hit each other, the hit produces gamma rays and other types of radiation. Gamma rays are dangerous because they can kill living cells. Yet controlled radiation saves human lives. Doctors use gamma rays to kill some types of cancer cells. They direct radiation to the affected part of the patient's body. Killing the cancer cells may help healthy cells grow in their place. Doctors can also use gamma radiation to help them spot certain cancers.

Strange but True

Scientists believe that gamma rays are coming at Earth from distant galaxies. Earth's atmosphere shields us from most rays produced in deep space.

25

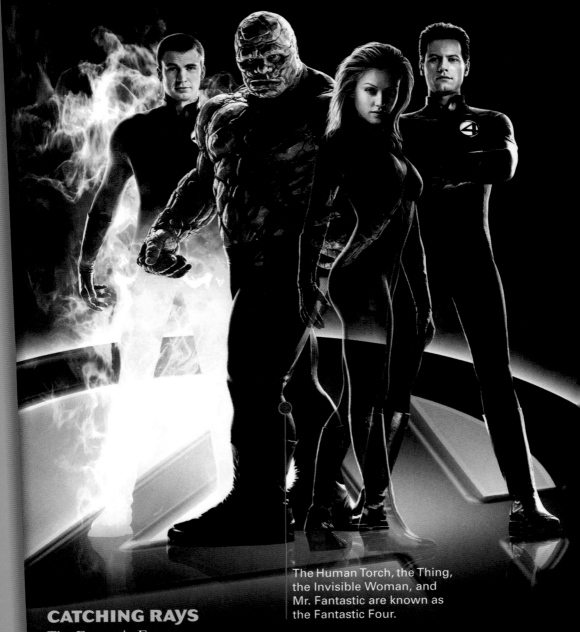

The Human Torch, the Thing, the Invisible Woman, and Mr. Fantastic are known as the Fantastic Four.

CATCHING RAYS

The Fantastic Four were once normal. Then Reed Richards, Ben Grimm, and Sue and Johnny Storm were hit by space rays during a test flight. The radiation caused big changes in their bodies. Reed gained the ability to stretch his body and change shape. Johnny became able to cover his body in fire and fly. Sue could make herself invisible. Ben developed superhuman strength. The superheroes use their fantastic powers to fight evil.

INSIDE A CELL

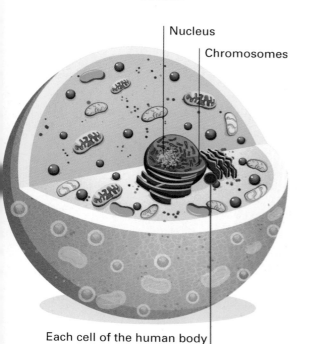

Nucleus

Chromosomes

Each cell of the human body contains genetic material.

POWER OF CHANGE

Cells are tiny body parts with certain jobs. A cell's nucleus, or center, is sometimes called its "brain." It directs the cell's activity. Within the nucleus are **chromosomes**. These rod-shaped parts contain all the genes a person got from both parents. Genes decide features such as hair color and eye color.

Radiation can cause genes to mutate. Even the Sun's rays can cause mutations. Certain chemicals can cause changes, too. Sometimes, genes even mutate by accident. Simple mistakes can happen when the cell copies itself and divides in two.

FROM MUTATION TO ADAPTATION

Some mutations cause physical changes that are passed down from parents to offspring. The changes that "stick" are **adaptations**. They are the features that help an organism do well in its environment. Features that do not aid survival slowly disappear.

Living things **evolve**, or change continually, over a long time. Creatures are adapted for the places they live and the things they do. For example, fish have gills to remove oxygen from water. Birds have hollow bones that are light enough for flight. Humans have adaptations, too. People from cold regions, for instance, tend to have long noses. Their noses can warm air longer when they breathe in.

Super Sticky

When Peter Parker was bitten by a radioactive spider, he changed into Spider-Man. He could suddenly cling to almost any surface.

Geckos have developed the same ability. Tiny "hairs" on their feet let the creatures climb walls and panes of glass. Scientists are studying geckos to find ways for people to do the same thing. A human-size Spider-Man suit could be a reality soon—thanks to science!

THE OUTSIDE STORY

Arthropods, such as lobsters, crabs, and spiders, developed skeletons on the outside of their bodies. A skeleton on the outside of the body is called an **exoskeleton**. This adaptation allows the creatures to live in tough environments.

An exoskeleton is like a suit of armor. It protects an animal's soft body. On land, the hard covering keeps the body from drying out. An exoskeleton also protects against **predators**.

Even though an exoskeleton is hard, it can bend so that the animal can move. An exoskeleton cannot grow as the animal gets bigger, however. An arthropod sheds its exoskeleton as it grows. This process is dangerous for the animal because its soft body parts are uncovered for a time.

What do exoskeletons have to do with superheroes? Some superheroes have exoskeletons of their own!

Strange but True

Can you imagine an army of Iron Man soldiers? Scientists and engineers are working to outfit U.S. soldiers with robot suits. The high-tech exoskeletons would improve their strength and speed. The fighters could carry hundreds of pounds. They could also leap high and far. Does this sound like science fiction? The inventor of the robot exoskeleton says comic books give him ideas for real-world technology.

Protected by a high-tech exoskeleton, Iron Man fights for justice.

Tony Stark is a billionaire scientist. Villains capture him and try to force him to build a killer weapon. Instead, he builds a suit of armor and escapes. Back home, Stark adds high-tech upgrades to his exoskeleton. His new Iron Man suit gives him superstrength and protection. The suit also enables him to fly. It includes state-of-the-art weapons and communication devices.

WHAT DO YOU THINK?

What other animal adaptations might inspire scientists and inventors to create new technology?

Super SENSES

The five basic senses are sight, sound, smell, touch, and taste. Spider-Man has an extra sense, called "spidey sense." He gets a tingling feeling that tells him when danger is near. Many superheroes have extra-sharp senses. Your senses are pretty amazing, too!

NOW, HEAR THIS!

The Bionic Woman's bionic ear lets her hear sounds that are very far away. She can also focus on a single sound in a noisy place.

Human hearing is super, too. You hear sounds because your ears and **nervous system** work together. Sound moves as waves through the air. The outer ear collects sound waves and carries them toward the middle ear. Sound waves hit the **eardrum**. The movement of the eardrum passes to the inner ear, which sends a signal to the brain. The brain "reads" the signal. That is how we tell a dog bark from a car horn.

HEARING HELP

A "bionic ear" of sorts is helping some people with severe hearing loss. A doctor places a small electronic part in the patient's ear. A tiny microphone outside the ear picks up sound. The

"Seeing" Sound

Daredevil is a superhero who lost his sense of sight. He "sees" by using sound waves to figure out where things are. The waves bounce off objects around him. He senses the waves and knows how close the objects are. Bats hear the same way! The process is called **echolocation**.

sound is sent to a "mini computer" that changes the sound into electric signals. Those signals then go to the device inside the ear, called an **implant**. The implant picks up the signal. It works the way a radio picks up a signal from a radio station. The implant then sends a signal to the brain, which makes sense of it.

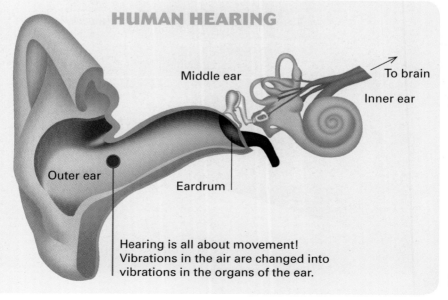

HUMAN HEARING

Middle ear

To brain

Inner ear

Outer ear

Eardrum

Hearing is all about movement! Vibrations in the air are changed into vibrations in the organs of the ear.

SEEING THE LIGHT

Is there something on the other side of a wall? No problem! Superman can see through it. Superman has **X-ray** vision. Humans do not. We see only **visible light**. Yet the human eye is a super organ!

X-RAY VISION FOR YOU?

Scientists in Scotland are working on eyeglasses that could give people super sight! The glasses create an image similar to an X-ray. The wearer can see through cloth, paper, and plastics. How? The glasses give off special beams of light. The beams bounce off the object being viewed. Then the beams return to the glasses to create a picture on the inside of the lens.

Catch the Waves

Radio waves	waves that carry signals for televisions, radios, and cell phones
Microwaves	waves that heat food in microwave ovens
Infrared waves	waves that we experience as heat
Visible light	the only waves people can see
Ultraviolet rays	waves emitted by the Sun. Some insects, like bees, can see them!
X-rays	rays used to take X-ray images
Gamma rays	waves that can kill living cells

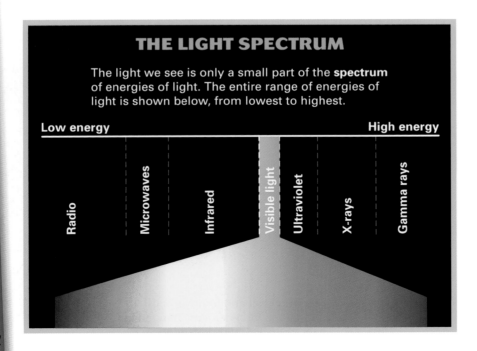

THE LIGHT SPECTRUM

The light we see is only a small part of the **spectrum** of energies of light. The entire range of energies of light is shown below, from lowest to highest.

Low energy — High energy

Radio | Microwaves | Infrared | Visible light | Ultraviolet | X-rays | Gamma rays

THE HUMAN EYE

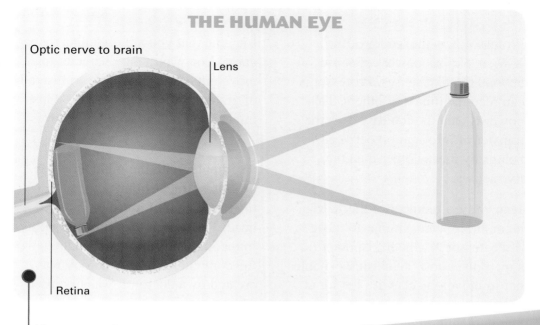

Optic nerve to brain

Lens

Retina

Your eyes and your brain team up so you get the picture.

IN PLAIN SIGHT

Light reflected off an object enters through the **pupil**. That is an opening at the front of the eye. The **lens** focuses the light (see diagram). The light then hits an inner layer of the eye called the **retina**. The image that reaches the retina is upside down. Chemicals in the retina change the light into electrical signals. Those signals travel along the **optic nerve** to the brain. The brain then reads the signals as visual images—right side up!

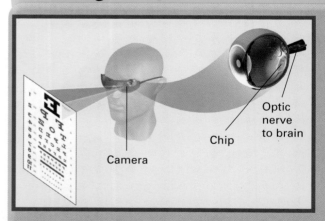

Strange but True

Optic nerve to brain

Chip

Camera

Scientists have also designed a bionic eye implant. The device could let many blind people see again. A tiny computer part, called a **chip**, sits behind the eye. The chip is the size of a pencil eraser. The chip links to a mini video camera built into special glasses. The camera beams pictures to the chip, which sends a message to the brain. The person sees an image!

PSYCHIC POWERS

Professor X is the leader of the X-Men. He has powers of sense beyond the five senses. Professor X can read the minds of others. This power is called **telepathy**. It is the transfer of information between beings by means other than the five senses.

Jean Gray, a member of the X-Men team, has powers similar to those of Professor X. She has another superpower, too. **Telekinesis** enables her to move objects with her mind. The powers of the mind are more real than you might think.

MIND OVER MATTER

Imagine that you are playing a video game. You want your character to move out of the way of a car. Instead of grabbing for the control, you just think about it. The character moves!

A new device lets players control a computer with the mind alone. A headband tracks brain activity and the movement of muscles in the head. The device then turns thoughts into commands and sends them to the computer. The technology was created by a doctor. It was first used in medicine.

Special senses give the X-Men team superpowers.

34

YOU DO IT!

Test Your Psychic Ability

What You Need
- 25 cards of the same color and size
- marker or pen
- friend

What You Do
Step 1

Make a deck of cards. Draw five very different shapes on five separate cards. Copy each card so your deck has five of each.

Step 2

Shuffle the cards. Have a friend pull a card from the deck, look at it, and try to "send" you the image on the card with his or her mind. Can you get the signal?

Step 3

Shuffle the deck. Place the cards facedown. Guess which card is on top. Turn it over. Was your prediction correct? Continue guessing as you flip the cards.

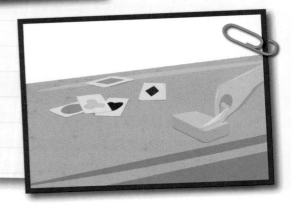

What Happened?
Some people are better than others at guessing!

Chapter 7

Hidden FROM VIEW

The leaf-tailed gecko is almost "invisible" in its surroundings.

ou are carrying your lunch tray in the school cafeteria. You trip. Your lunch flies everywhere. At that moment, you wish you could disappear from sight, just like the Invisible Woman . . . and certain animals, too!

SIGHT UNSEEN

Light waves bounce off objects. When the waves reach a viewer's eyes, the viewer sees the objects. The Invisible Woman bends light waves around herself. She stays hidden because the waves do not bounce off her.

CLOAKED IN INVISIBILITY

Do you ever wish you could disappear? Someday soon, you might be able to do just that! Researchers in the United States have invented an "invisibility coat." The material uses heat to bend light rays around an object.

Japanese scientists are at work on a similar suit. It is made of a special material that works like a movie screen. A camera on the suit takes a picture of whatever is behind the wearer. That picture is projected onto the front of the suit. Looking at the front, you see what is behind instead. With a special coat, shoes, gloves, and hood, a person could disappear from sight.

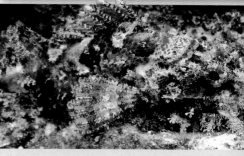

Critter Camouflage

How do some animals make themselves invisible to enemies? They use **camouflage**. Color and pattern help them blend in with their surroundings. Some fish, for example, are the same colors and patterns as coral or plants in the ocean. When a bigger fish is on the lookout for a meal, the smaller fish can easily stay hidden. Patterns help land animals blend in, too. For example, a tiger's stripes make the big cat hard to spot in tall grass.

Now you see the coat . . . now you don't!

MYSTIQUE

One time you see her, she looks like a prison guard. Another time, she is a U.S. senator. Who is she? She is Mystique, a villain who fights the X-Men. She has the special power of shape-shifting. That power comes in handy in the world of comic book superheroes. It is helpful in the animal world, too.

SHAPE-SHIFTERS

Some animals go through **metamorphosis**. They change at different stages in life. A tiny tadpole turns into a big green frog. A caterpillar becomes a moth or a butterfly.

Some animals can change their shapes to protect themselves. When an enemy is near, some toads and snakes puff themselves up to appear larger. A fish called the puffer can make itself appear three times larger to scare off attackers. The fish inflates by pumping water into its stomach.

This fish gets "pumped up" when an enemy threatens.

MASTERS OF DISGUISE

Animals with camouflage blend into their surroundings. What if the surroundings are also changing? Some animals can change color to blend in with whatever surrounds them. In spring and summer, the arctic fox has a brown coat that matches its environment. In fall and winter, the fox's fur turns white. The fox can then blend in with the snow. The ability to change color helps keep the animal hidden.

The octopus has special cells in its skin that can change color. Most kinds of octopuses have three or four colors in their skin. They use their color to hide. They also use their color to communicate with other octopuses! Octopuses can also use skin muscles to change the skin's texture. It can look like seaweed or take on the bumpy texture of rocks.

WHAT DO YOU THINK?

Which "superpower" is more valuable in the animal world: color camouflage or shape changing? Explain your choice.

An octopus can change the color and texture of its skin.

Chapter 8

Super
SCIENTISTS

Scientists answer questions about the world around us. Some scientists warn us of bad weather. Others help cure diseases. In the comic book world, scientists can be superheroes or villains. Knowledge is a powerful tool. It can change the world for better or worse.

The evil Lex Luthor is Superman's archenemy.

Evil genius Dr. Doom wears a metal mask to cover his face. It was blasted by cosmic rays.

BAD SCIENCE

There is no shortage of mad scientists in the comic book world. Lex Luthor, Superman's worst enemy, is a brilliant inventor gone bad. He uses his scientific genius for evil. This villain tries again and again to kill Superman and take over the world.

DOOMSDAY

Dr. Doom is another scientist with super smarts. Unfortunately, he uses his brainpower against the Fantastic Four, the Silver Surfer, and other superheroes. With a wide knowledge of technology, Doom has created a time machine. He has also built an army of robotic "Doombots" to do his dirty work.

THE DARK SIDE

Otto Octavius was a respected scientist until an accident changed his life for the worse. Octavius had designed a set of robot arms in his lab. An explosion fused the mechanical arms to his body. Radiation caused changes to his brain, so he could control the robot arms with his mind. Dr. Octopus then turned to a life of crime.

THE GOOD GUYS

In contrast to the bad guys, some superhero scientists have a heart. Bruce Wayne, for example, is the superhero Batman. He is a wealthy man without superpowers. Yet he knows science and technology. His knowledge and money help him build high-tech gadgets. He has built everything from wall-climbing devices to the Batmobile, the Batboat, and the Batcycle.

A FANTASTIC MIND

Reed Richards leads the Fantastic Four. Known as Mr. Fantastic, he is one of the most intelligent superheroes. He can face almost any challenge with his knowledge of chemistry, biology, and engineering. In the superhero world, Reed makes major scientific discoveries. He knows about space travel, time travel, robots, computers, and mutation. He can even figure out languages from other worlds!

In real life, most scientists work in one branch of science. Many scientists do amazing things. They study the world and make it better, one project at a time.

What about you? If you were a scientist, how might you use your knowledge to be a real-life superhero?

THE BAT-BELT

Holy Bat-gear! The Caped Crusader has some cool crime-fighting gadgets.

CAMERA!
Batman's mini camera has a polarized Bat-filter.

TRACER!
Batman uses the tracer to track down villains.

MEDICAL KIT!
Even Batman is prepared to fight injuries!

BATARANG!
This razor-sharp weapon takes down bad guys.

DARTS!
Sharp darts tipped with chemicals knock out crooks on the run.

BAT-BOLAS!
When he needs to trip up an enemy, Batman tosses the bolas.

BAT-CUFFS!
Criminals are no match for Batman's special cuffs.

43

SCIENCE AT WORK

SIGNAL PROCESSING ENGINEER

Job Description: Engineers use principles of science to solve technical problems. They use science to meet the needs of society and consumers. Many engineers develop new products.

Job Outlook: Overall opportunities are good.
Earnings: $53,910 to $135,260, with a median income of $88,470

Source: Bureau of Labor Statistics

Conversation With a Scientist and Inventor

Kevin Fisher designs chips for DSL modems. Those devices connect computers to the Internet.

WHAT HAVE YOU INVENTED?

Before I started designing DSL modem chips, I designed chips that go into hard disk drives for PCs [personal computers] and laptops. These chips made it possible to store more [information].

WHAT DID YOU NEED TO STUDY TO DO THE JOB?

When I was a kid, I really liked math. My job allows me to use math and science to solve important problems that will benefit people.

WHAT DO YOU LIKE MOST ABOUT YOUR WORK?

I like solving challenging problems that other people said were impossible to solve.

WHAT IS MOST CHALLENGING ABOUT YOUR CAREER?

It is necessary to keep learning, growing, and adapting to the changing situation.

IF I WERE INTERESTED IN HAVING A CAREER LIKE YOURS, WHAT ADVICE WOULD YOU GIVE ME?

If you think solving math and science problems is fun, then you may be well suited for engineering. Don't be afraid of making mistakes. If you challenge yourself, you will make mistakes. When it happens, learn from your mistakes and move on. Learn how to work in a team of other people. Engineering projects are too complicated for a single person to do them alone.

FIND OUT MORE

BOOKS

Christiansen, Jeff, et al. *All-New Official Handbook of the Marvel Universe A to Z.* New York: Marvel Comics, 2008.

Reeves, Diane Lindsey, and Lindsey Clasen. *Career Ideas for Kids Who Like Science.* New York: Chelsea House Publishers, 2007.

Wolf, Steve. *The Secret Science Behind Movie Stunts and Special Effects.* New York: Skyhorse Publishing, 2007.

WEB SITES

Clearwater Marine Aquarium
www.seewinter.com
See Winter, the bottlenose dolphin with a prosthetic tail, in action.

Science Channel
science.discovery.com/videos/kapow-superhero-science-magnetic-levitation.html
Watch researchers use magnets to make some super science of their own!

Superhero Science Quiz for Kids
www.funtrivia.com/trivia-quiz/ForChildren/Superhero-Science-264968.html
How much do you know about the science behind superpowers? Take this quiz to find out!

GLOSSARY

adaptations: adjustments to conditions in the environment that improve an organism's chance of survival

arthropods: animals with a hard outer shell, such as crabs

atoms: the smallest known components of an element

bionic: having to do with body parts changed with electronic or mechanical parts

camouflage: a way that animals conceal, or hide, themselves with color, pattern, or texture

cells: small, complicated units that form plant and animal tissues

chemical energy: the energy made available by chemical changes

chip: a small electronic part that is one of the basic elements of most electronic devices

chromosomes: the structures in cells that contain DNA

drag: the force that slows forward movement as a body moves through a fluid such as air

eardrum: a tiny structure that works like a drum within the ear

echolocation: the ability to send out sound waves that bounce off objects so the sender can "hear" the objects' locations

evolve: to change over time

exoskeleton: a hard outer shell that is the skeleton of some animals

friction: the resistance to movement that happens when two things rub or slide against each other

gamma rays: tiny units of a plant or animal cell that determine the characteristics an offspring inherits from its parent or parents

genes: the specific sequence of DNA in a cell

gravity: the force that attracts objects toward the center of Earth or another space body

implant: a material or device inserted into the body

lens: the part of the eye that focuses light

lift: a force that opposes weight to lift an object moving through air

light waves: radiation in the form of waves of different sizes, some of which are visible to the eye

magnetism: the force that attracts or repels magnets and magnetic materials

mechanical energy: the energy of motion used to do work

metamorphosis: the process through which certain animals change form from birth to adult

MRI: magnetic resonance imaging; a manner of making an image

mutations: new genetic features in an organism

nervous system: the body system that includes the brain, spinal cord, and nerves

nuclear physicist: one who studies the branch of science having to do with atoms and their parts

nucleus: (1) the central portion of an atom; (2) the part of a cell that tells it what to do

optic nerve: either of the nerves that connect one eye to the brain

predators: animals that feed on other animals

prostheses: artificial body parts

pupil: in the human eye, the black center opening that lets in light

radiation: energy given off in the form of waves or very tiny particles

radioactive: giving off particles or rays that escape from an atom

retina: the lining inside the eyeball that receives images from the lens and that changes them into signals to be sent to the brain

satellites: objects that circle other objects, especially in space

sound waves: waves of pressure that travel in air, act on the ear, and make sound possible

spectrum: an ordered arrangement by a particular characteristic, such as energy or frequency

telekinesis: the power to move objects with one's mind

telepathy: the power to read or influence another person's mind

teleport: to move matter by changing it from one form of energy to another

thrust: a force that moves something in flight forward

visible light: waves of light that can be seen by the eye

X-ray: an unseen form of radiation that can pass through body tissue and like materials

INDEX

About the Authors

Lynnette Brent Sandvold has taught science and reading, and she has written science books about matter, chemistry, light, heat, and science experiments you can do at home. Ms. Sandvold loves superheroes and has met many of them at comic book conventions. She watches superhero films at home with her husband, her two amazing sons, and two cats.

Barbara Bakowski has worked in children's book and magazine publishing for more than 20 years. She dedicates this book to her own superheroes, Taffy the Wonder Dog and his sidekick, Fat Trixie.